AL'S WORLD
MONDAY MORNING BLITZ

AL'S WORLD
MONDAY MORNING BLITZ

BOOK 1

Elise Leonard

ALADDIN PAPERBACKS
NEW YORK   LONDON   TORONTO   SYDNEY

ALADDIN PAPERBACKS
An imprint of Simon & Schuster Children's Publishing Division
1230 Avenue of the Americas, New York, NY 10020
Copyright © 2007 by Elise Leonard
All rights reserved, including the right of reproduction in whole or in part in any form.
ALADDIN PAPERBACKS and related logo are registered trademarks of Simon & Schuster, Inc.
Designed by Christopher Grassi
The text of this book was set in Berkeley Old Style.
Manufactured in the United States of America
First Aladdin Paperbacks edition June 2007
10 9 8 7 6 5 4 3 2 1
Library of Congress Control Number 2006936000
ISBN-13: 978-1-4169-3464-6
ISBN-10: 1-4169-3464-2

ACKNOWLEDGMENTS

Special thanks to Rubin Pfeffer for having an open mind. As Al would say, "For a suit, you're pretty cool."

This series would not be here without the extraordinary talent (and great taste) of Julia Richardson. Thank you, Julia. You are not only Al and Keith's fairy godmother, you are mine too. We're so lucky to have you!

For Molly McGuire: You got thrown right into the fire, but came out better than a perfectly toasted marshmallow. In my book, there's not much better than that! You're an excellent editor and I'm so happy to be working with you. Thank you for all you've done so far, and for all you will continue to do. Al, Keith, and I are fortunate to have fallen into your very capable hands.

To my sons Michael and John: Keep charging at life head-on. I've still got your backs.

To my husband John: You are my anchor. Without you, I'd be adrift.

To my readers: Thanks for choosing the first book of the AL'S WORLD series. I hope you like it! Each book in the series is different, but they're all funny. (Mostly because Al and Keith are in them.)

Oh, and hopefully this will be the last serious acknowledgements page I do. (I'm sorry everybody, but it's my first one for the series, so I'm trying to sound important and intelligent. So please cut me some slack. Okay?)

~Elise

CHAPTER

1

W hat's that thing on your face?" Keith asked me.
I took a shot in the dark. "My nose?"

"No," Keith said. "That other thing."

I hadn't had time to look in the mirror this morning, so I had no idea what he was talking about. "What other thing?"

"The 'other thing' that looks like you're trying to grow an other nose on your forehead."

I reached up and touched my forehead, feeling around.

Oh, no! I knew it the minute my fingers hit the large bump. I had a pimple. A big pimple. A *huge* pimple, really. I had a zit the size of Mount Fuji. Great.

"How could you not notice that, Al?" Keith asked.

"I didn't look in the mirror this morning," I said as I leaned close to Keith to catch my reflection in his glasses.

"Yeah, I get that now," he said as he pushed me away. "You didn't brush your teeth either. Did you?!"

I huffed into my cupped hand and sniffed it. "No. Sorry."

Keith shrugged. "I only have one word for you. Breath mint!"

"That's two words," I said, trying not to show that I was embarrassed.

Keith handed me an orange Tic Tac.

"Have any cinnamon?" I asked.

He pushed my hand with the Tic Tac to my

face. "No. I don't. Do I *look* like a candy store?" he asked. "Just eat it, Al. Take my word. You need it."

"But I'm not a big fan of orange," I said truthfully.

"I'm not a big fan of your stinky breath. Just eat the thing."

I popped it in my mouth. It didn't taste that bad. It didn't taste that good, either. But that's only because I just don't like orange flavor. I think it goes back to when I was a kid. Every time I got sick, my mom would give me this gross orange-flavored medicine. I gagged on it every time and used to wonder what was worse: the cold or the cure.

"Hey, get a load of that," Keith said, pointing to a man running down the street. He was heading our way. Fast.

If he were wearing sweats, it wouldn't have looked so funny. But he was wearing a suit and tie and shiny black shoes. I could see their shine all the way from where I stood, so they *had* to be really shiny.

"You think he's running *to* something, or running *away* from something?" I asked aloud.

I hadn't expected an answer, I was just thinking out loud.

I do that a lot. You know, talk to myself. I call it "thinking out loud" because that sounds better than saying I'm a nutcase who talks to himself.

The guy was running toward us as if his life depended upon it. He was about five feet away when he looked over his shoulder.

Keith and I tried to get out of his way and moved over, but he wasn't looking forward. That would explain why he crashed right into me—knocking me over.

I landed on my backpack, and one of my books stabbed me in the ribs. "Ow!" I cried out.

"Why don't you look where you're going?" Keith said to the guy.

I doubt he heard Keith because the man was already halfway down the block. But he did look back quickly, wave, and call out, "Sorry!"

I got up and was just straightening out my jacket when I felt a lump in my pocket. It was probably my rib. I was too afraid to find out. I'm not too keen on blood, especially when it's my own.

I don't mind seeing blood in the movies. That's pretty cool. Plus, everyone knows it's just ketchup or something. But real blood? Let's just say my firm C-minus average wasn't the only thing keeping me from medical school.

"That really hurt," I said to Keith. I was trying not to think about the rib poking through my skin at an odd angle. I couldn't even look to see if blood was pouring out of me. I figured if it was, someone would let me know sooner or later.

The bus pulled up, and we grabbed our stuff to get on. If we didn't get on the bus fast enough,

Mrs. Sewers, the bus driver, took off without us.

"Oh man, this hurts," I said with a groan as I lifted my heavy backpack.

"Quit your griping," Keith said.

"But it hurt! He knocked the wind out of me. I'm having trouble catching my breath," I said truthfully. I wondered if my broken rib pierced a lung or something. That couldn't be good.

"Well, what do you want from me? Mouth-to-mouth? Not with *that* breath."

I pushed him up the stairs of the bus.

"Hey! No foul play, boys!" Mrs. Sewers barked. She was like the drill sergeant of bus drivers. "Not on *my* bus!" she added as a warning. It was warning enough. *No one* messed with Mrs. Sewers. Rumor had it, she was called Mrs. Sewers because she *grew up* in the sewers. She was one tough old lady. And few people messed with her.

"I have a perfect safety record, and you hooligans aren't going to ruin it for me!" she said gruffly.

She worried about her safety record. A lot. She'd been driving a bus for twenty years without one incident, and she was proud of that.

"'Hooligans'?" Keith asked. "Who says 'hooligans'?"

I shrugged, then regretted the movement. The pain in my rib felt like a knife going through me. Well, what I'd *think* a knife going through me would feel like. Not good.

We took our assigned seats. Luckily, Keith and I were assigned to the same bench. We kids always thought it was stupid to have assigned seats on a bus, but it was another one of Mrs. Sewers's safety rules.

It was always quiet on the bus in the mornings. At that hour, most of us were still half asleep.

When we got to school, everyone piled off the bus.

I held my backpack in my hand because my

rib still hurt. So of course as I walked down the crowded hallway, some guy clipped my side. When I rubbed it, that's when I felt the thing that kept stabbing into me.

CHAPTER

2

I turned to face Keith head-on and pointed to where it hurt. "Do me a favor, will ya?"

"Sure. Anything, bud. What do you need?" he asked.

"Just tell me if I'm dying," I said softly.

Keith stared at me.

Then he shrugged. "How am *I* supposed to know?"

"Am I bleeding badly?" I croaked pitifully.

He looked around my middle.

"Nope," he said calmly.

"Just average?" I whispered.

"Nope," he repeated.

"At *all*?" I wailed.

"Nope again," he said.

"You probably just can't see it," I said weakly.

"If I can't *see* it, Al, then you're not bleeding," he said firmly.

"It's probably internal," I muttered to myself.

Yeah, that's right. When I die of internal bleeding, won't *he* feel stupid for arguing with me!

"I think there's something in my jacket stabbing me," I said.

I took off my jacket and threw it at him.

Well, I tried to throw it at him.

I was off by about two feet.

The jacket fell on the ground with a small *clink*.

"You have money in there?" he asked.

"Do I *ever* have money in there?"

Keith laughed and shook his head. "No. You're always sponging off of me."

I looked at him, and he looked at me. "So what do you think that thing is in there?" I asked.

"How should I know?" Keith asked with a loud sigh. "You think I can see through fabric?"

"Just feel around in there, would you?" I asked. He was getting really annoying.

He bent over and got the jacket. First, he straightened it out, then he held it up in front of himself. He was holding it up at the top—by the collar. Then he started squeezing it from the top to the bottom. Like he was trying to empty all the toothpaste from a tube.

I watched him perform his tidy check.

On second thought, he looked like he was trying to milk a cow.

"What are you *doing*?" I demanded.

"I'm checking," he said. "Like you asked me to do!"

"So? Do you *feel* anything?" He looked like he was having *way* too much fun with my jacket.

"Yup, here it is," he said.

His hand was squeezing in the lower area of my jacket.

"What is it?" I asked.

"I don't have X-ray vision, and I don't have Braille hands," he said, starting to look as annoyed with me as I was with him.

Now he was laying my jacket on the floor and patting it down. "I feel it, but I can't get to it."

"It's not in the pocket?" I asked.

"If it were in the pocket, would I be doing all of this to try to get it out? I'd just reach in and take it out of the pocket, don't you think?" he asked.

I tried to bend over to help him with the jacket, but my rib was killing me. "Look. I can't help you down there. Let's go to your locker and we can open it up, and then we can hang the jacket from the corner of the locker."

Keith smiled. "That's brilliant!"

"Yeah. I'm going to be the next Albert Einstein," I said as we started walking to his locker.

We did just what I mentioned and between the two of us, we managed to move the long, skinny metal thing around the coat.

"There's a hole in this pocket," Keith said.

"That's new, because I never had any holes in my pockets before."

Keith was working hard. "Well, there's one now. Whatever this thing is, it slipped through the hole in your pocket and is in between the lining and the fabric of your coat."

He was fishing the thing around by holding it through the lining and catching it with his other hand from the outside of my jacket. "This is kind if fun," Keith said.

He's easily amused.

I'm not.

"Just get the thing out, would ya?!" I said.

"Sure, Al. I'm working on it."

Of course that was the exact time Shreena Gupta chose to walk by.

As always, Keith got all excited and waved. "Hey, Shreena," he called out.

As always, she barely noticed him. She smiled weakly and waved back and said a soft "hi," but there wasn't any passion in it. If you know what I mean.

But that never stopped Keith.

The metal thing had slipped back down to the bottom of the jacket again while he had stopped to wave.

"Oh, dang it. Now I have to start all over again," he said. He grinned at me as he started working the metal thing through the jacket again. Shreena Gupta did that to him. Made him goofy. Well, goofier than he usually was.

"Things aren't going too well with Shreena, huh?"

"Nah," he said. "But I have confidence that I'll break her down. I think she's already starting to soften up a bit."

"Yeah," I said. "I could really see that." I tried not to roll my eyes. It must be nice living in Keith-land.

"Got it!" he said. He pulled the thing out of my pocket and held it up.

"Cool," I said.

"Yeah," he said as we both stared at the long, metal thing.

People were pushing and shoving all around us, but we were just standing there staring at the long, thin, metal thing.

"So what do you think it is?" he asked.

"Beats me," I said.

"Maybe it's an alien device," Keith said with wide eyes.

I rolled my eyes and shook my head. "Yeah. That was my first guess too."

"It was?"

"No, Keith. It's not an alien device. I have no idea *what* it is, but I'm pretty sure it's not an alien device. You watch too much *Stargate*!"

"Hey, it's a cool show," he said in his defense.

"Can we *please* try to stay on topic here?"

Just then, some big dude bumped into Keith and knocked the metal thing out of his hand. It landed with a sharp *clink* and broke in half when it hit the tile floor.

CHAPTER

3

"Oh, great!" Kevin whined. "Now our 'alien device' is broken."

"However will we get home, Dorothy?" I said with a loud gasp.

"Oh my God, it's affecting you already," Keith said, looking worried. "I'm not Dorothy, Al, I'm Keith."

I smacked him upside the head. "I *know* that! I was pretending we were in the Land of Oz."

Keith stared at me.

"You know. *The Wizard of Oz?* Dorothy and her little dog Toto?"

When he still had that blank look, I shook my head. "Oh, forget it! I was just making a joke. It was totally wasted on you."

"Cool flash drive," some guy said. "Better pick it up before someone steps on it," he said over his shoulder as he kept walking.

"Ohhh, it's a flash drive," Keith and I said at the same time.

Keith picked it up and looked at it.

"A flash drive disguised as a knifey thing," Keith said while nodding his head. "That's a cool disguise."

"I think it's supposed to look like a letter opener. You know, like people have at work for their desks. That way it has an excuse for being near a computer."

"Good thinking, Al," Keith said, still nodding.

"Yeah, well, it's a hard job, but someone's got to do it," I cracked back.

"So what do you think this is for?" Keith asked as he looked closely at the long, skinny, metallic flash drive.

"I'd have to take a wild guess and say . . . storing some computer info?"

"Ya think?" Keith asked.

I rolled my eyes and shook my head. "It's a flash drive, Keith. What *else* do you think it would be used for?" I took the drive from his hand and looked at it. "That guy must've shoved it in my pocket as he fell on me. No wonder it felt like I'd been stabbed. In a way . . . I was. With *this* thing."

"It couldn't be very important if the guy just gave it away," Keith said.

Keith's not the sharpest tool in the shed. "Um, Keith? Did you ever think maybe the *opposite* is true?"

When he was still staring at me blankly, I went on.

"Maybe it *is* important. Very important. *So*

important that he was running away from someone who wanted what was on this thing."

"Wow. Cool," Keith said, getting into the story.

"Maybe he saw me and thought, *Now there's a guy I can trust. If I crash into him and slip it to him, he'll know what to do with it.*"

"So what should we do with it?" Keith asked eagerly.

I shrugged. "Beats me."

What? You thought *I'd* know what to do with it? I can't even set my alarm clock so I have time to brush my teeth in the morning. Do you *really* think I'd know what to do with a mysterious flash drive that may have, I don't know, world *secrets* on it or something? Like I told you. My average is a C minus. And you're thinking *I* should know what to do with something like this?

All I can say is, the next time that guy finds himself in a bad spot and needs to dump his high-tech secret-info knife on someone, he should do a little research first and give it to someone who'd know what to do with it. Like, say, John Larson. He's the smartest guy in the school.

"Hey," I said to Keith. "That's who we need."

"Who?" Keith asked.

"John Larson."

"Yeah, he's smart. Good idea, Al."

John's not in any of my classes (for obvious reasons), but I knew he was in the homeroom next to mine. "Let's go," I said, heading for my homeroom.

When we got to my homeroom, we went one door over and walked inside the classroom.

John was sitting at a desk, doing something with his calculator. It looked like he was playing a video game by the way his fingers were moving, but that couldn't be. It was a calculator. And handheld video games weren't allowed at school. I heard the principal had more video games locked in his office than all the Wal-Marts put together. He could open up his own store and make a mint. Instead, he just took 'em, tagged 'em, and gave 'em back at the end of the year.

We walked up behind John and I could see he *was* playing a video game. On his calculator! "Hey that's cool, man," I said.

John looked up, then looked around to see if anyone was listening. Like, for example, the homeroom teacher. When he saw no one was paying attention to us, he answered. "Yeah, I downloaded a few games on here to keep me busy during the down time," he said with a grin.

John was really smart, but he was nice, too. Not like the other geeks in the school. They were really stuck-up. Especially the girls. The smart girls wouldn't give me the time of day. Which was fine with me. They didn't need me, and I didn't need them. But I *did* need John.

I took out the flash drive and slipped it on his

desk. I covered it with one of John's books so the teacher wouldn't see. All I needed was to get in trouble for having a knife at school. Or a knife-like weapon. Of course I could prove it wasn't really a knife, but I'd rather not go through all that. "Ever seen one of these?" I asked John.

CHAPTER
4

For a second he turned pale. Like I was threatening him or something. But then I reached toward the flash drive and took the top off.

"Oh," John said with a small sigh of relief. "It's a flash drive. For a second there, I thought you were dangerous."

That made me laugh. "Me? Dangerous?" I laughed again.

Keith thought that was hilarious. "Al?" He looked at me. "*Dangerous? That's really* funny!"

I stopped laughing. It wasn't *that* funny. "Hey," I said to Keith, "I could be dangerous if I wanted to be. In fact, I'm starting to feel like getting dangerous now." I gave Keith my best "knock it off before I hurt you" look. Keith just grinned back.

"Ms. Parks, is it okay if I use one of your computers for a second?" John asked his homeroom teacher.

While Keith and I were fighting, John had moved over to the bank of computers. He had the flash drive with him.

"Sure, John," she said with a smile. She most likely knew that John would never hurt a computer. If anything, knowing John, it would run better after he used it than before.

John plugged the flash drive into the USB port, then clicked a few times on stuff to get it to open up. When it opened, the screen was filled with all sorts of symbols and stuff. Nothing you could read.

"Bummer, Al. It doesn't work. It's all messed up," Keith said, looking from the screen to me.

John laughed. "It's not messed up, guys. It's encrypted."

"You can read that?" Keith said with awe.

"No. Can you?" he asked Keith.

"No. But I'm not a brainiac like you," Keith said.

"I'm smart, but I'm not *that* smart." John looked at me. He probably wanted to have an intelligent conversation for a change. "The whole thing's encrypted, Al." He looked back at the computer and did a whole bunch of things, but the stuff on the screen stayed the same. "It's a really good encryption too. And I can't cut through it on this machine. I'll have to take the drive to the computer lab if you want me to decode it. We have software there that might help."

"Yeah, I want you to decode it. I want to know what I almost got killed for today," I said with a snort.

"You almost got killed today?" John asked, looking surprised.

I nodded, but Keith answered. "If you can call getting run down by a guy in a business suit almost getting killed."

Keith was annoying me again. "Hey! He hit *me*, not you, Keith. So until you get plowed down by a guy who's a lot harder and heavier than he looks, keep your opinion to yourself!"

Keith held up his hands in front of him. "Whoa, cool down, Al. I was only trying to lighten up the situation."

John was still trying to get through the code on the stuff in the flash drive. "I don't want to make you nervous or anything, guys, but this thing has been encrypted *multiple* times. Whoever had this information didn't want anyone else getting it."

"So he gave it to Al?" Keith snorted a laugh.

I threw Keith a look. "I have second period free. Study hall. Can I meet you at the computer lab then?" I asked John.

John thought about it for a moment. "Yeah, I can do that. I have chemistry, but I can get a pass out if I say it's important."

"You can *do* that?" I asked. No teacher of mine would do that for me. But perhaps that's because they don't think I'm all there when I *am* sitting in their classes. I guess they figure it's better to have me 60 percent there than not there at all. Heck, John probably gets more out of *not* being in class than I do when I *am* in class!

"Yeah. I'll make up the work," John said.

See what I mean? He'll actually make an effort to find out what they did in class when he was gone. Me? I'd figure, I wasn't there, I missed *that* boat, so I'd better get on the boat that *is* riding when I *am* there. No use confusing the issue by trying to learn something that happened while I wasn't there. Learning the stuff happening while I *am* there is hard enough.

"What do you want to do with the drive?" John asked Keith and me.

"How should I know?" Keith answered, and looked at me.

All eyes were on me. "How should *I* know?" I said.

"The guy put it in *your* pocket," Keith said.

"It could easily have been put in yours," I said to Keith.

"Yeah, but it wasn't," Keith shot back.

John sighed. "Um, guys? You only have four minutes left for homeroom. You'd better get there and check in. Why don't you keep the drive, Al? I'll meet you at the computer lab during second period."

Sounded like a plan.

Second period came quickly. John was coming from the opposite direction, so I could see him walking to the lab. I waited by the door until he got there. "Will I be allowed inside?" I asked.

"Yeah. No problem. We rule the place," John said with a smile.

"We do?" I asked, smiling back.

"We as in me and my friends, not we as in you and me."

He shoved the door open and was greeted by a whole bunch of smart kids who didn't even know my name.

"Hey all, this is Al," John said as he put his backpack on the floor next to a computer station.

"Hi, Al," they all chimed. It sounded like we were at an A.A. meeting.

"Hi," I said back, waving and smiling. This was the closest I'd ever gotten to a think tank and I was hoping some of their brains would seep out into me.

I guess there was no chance of *that* happening because as I was looking at the cool video game on some guy's screen, I tripped over a backpack and fell into a computer station. After I apologized to the surprised girl who was lying—crushed—beneath me, I got off of her and walked over to John.

I'm really good with first impressions.

CHAPTER
5

W hat do you mean he couldn't get through it?" Keith asked as we walked home from the bus stop.

"I mean, it's encrypted so well, he couldn't get through it," I said.

"But John's the smartest guy we know," Keith said. The way he said it, he made it seem like he thought that just because he'd said it, it would force things to go right.

"Yeah, he's the smartest guy we know, but

whoever encrypted that flash drive was as smart or smarter than John."

Keith turned pale at the thought that there were people out there smarter than John Larson. "That's scary," Keith said.

I shrugged. "He'll get through it in time."

"Are you a little afraid of what's on it?" Keith asked.

I hadn't really thought about it. I mean, it had to be important stuff, or it wouldn't be so well encrypted. It's not like anyone does that to a list of their favorite ice-cream flavors. Or a numbered list of someone's favorite actresses (in order of hotness—with number one being the world's hottest actress, and going down the list after that). At least I didn't *think* so. "Would you encrypt that list of actresses we made last summer?" I asked Keith.

Keith laughed. "Heck, no! I helped make that list and I'm proud of it! In fact, now that you've reminded me of that, we should get our own Web page and post it." He laughed out loud again. "*With* pictures!"

I just looked at Keith.

"I bet we'd get a *lot* of hits," he said with passion.

This was my right-hand man? *This* was the guy who was going to help me get through times of trouble? He couldn't even hold a serious thought.

"I'm not fooling around here, Keith. Try to stay with me, okay?" I looked at him squarely. "We were talking about the flash drive."

"Oh yeah, right," he said with a shy smile. "Sorry."

We walked along in silence.

"So where is it now?" Keith asked.

"I let John take it home so he could keep working on it. It's like a puzzle to him, and he really wants to solve it."

Keith shrugged. "Oh, all right. I guess that's okay. Good thing we have him on our side," Keith said.

"Yeah," was all I said back.

• • •

The next morning I'd managed to wake up early enough to brush my teeth, take a shower, stick a Band-Aid over my monster pimple, *and* have breakfast. Looked like it was going to be a good day. My ribs were still a tiny bit sore, but not much.

I got to the bus stop right after Keith got there.

"Hey. Look at you," Keith said with a smile. "No bed head. Which means . . . you showered."

"Thanks for noticing," I said while rolling my eyes.

Out of *nowhere*, the man from yesterday appeared like a shadow.

"Do you have the flash drive?" he asked from behind me. I could feel his hot breath on the back of my neck and I looked down to see his shiny shoes.

He scared me out of my wits. "I-I-I, uh . . ."

How was I going to explain that I'd given it to a smart friend so he could take a look at what was on it? Somehow, I didn't think this guy would find that of interest. In fact, it would probably make him mad. It was *his* flash drive, and he wanted it back.

Before I could answer (or come up with anything good in my defense), I heard a screeching sound as a car veered off the road. I looked up just in time to see it heading straight for the guy and me. I froze. Stunned. But suddenly I felt two hands on my back and I was shoved with a force like I've never felt before. If I'd been standing outside my body, I would have seen myself lurch a good twelve feet.

It all happened so fast, I was in a daze. But I remember hearing tires screech, a heavy thud, a woman scream, and a car taking off.

I got up and ran to the guy with the shiny shoes. He'd been hit by the car and was lying on the sidewalk. Exactly where I'd been standing.

His leg was bloody and sticking out in a way it shouldn't have been. And it was bent at a place that shouldn't be able to bend.

"Are you okay?" I asked the man.

Keith was just standing there staring. His mouth was hanging open, and his face was really pale.

"I think it's shattered," the man said as he crawled up on his elbows and managed to stand using only one leg. The other one hung down, useless, the toe pointing in a different direction from the unhurt leg. It was freaky.

Blood was oozing down his pant leg and pooling on the sidewalk. I was getting nauseated.

"You should probably sit down," I said.

"I'll be fine," he said as the sound of police cars came toward us from the distance.

"Are you okay?" he asked.

I snorted a laugh and tried not to look at all the blood. "Yeah. Thanks to you," I said with awe. "Thanks for that," I said seriously, pointing to where he'd shoved me out of the way.

I was still in a daze. Still flustered. Still a little shell-shocked.

"No problem," he said back to me. "Just do me a favor," he said, looking around as the sirens got closer.

"Yeah, sure," I said. "Anything." This guy had just saved my life; I'd do anything for him.

"Keep that drive safe," he said before he turned on his good foot and sort of hopped away. I saw his bad leg dragging behind him.

"You got it," I called to his back just before barfing up the entire breakfast I'd eaten about twenty minutes before.

Keith was still in shock, because all he said was, "I see you had eggs."

CHAPTER
6

The police pulled up just after that.

"You kids okay?" the cop who was driving asked as he jumped out of the car.

His partner ran to the sidewalk and looked at the big pool of blood.

"You all right?" he asked quickly, looking at us from top to bottom to see where we were hurt.

"It's not my blood," I said to the two officers.

Another cop car showed up with a screech. The officers jumped out and ran over.

"It's not the kid's blood," the first guy said to the new crew to bring them up to speed.

"But it's his barf," Keith volunteered. "Look," he said pointing to it. "He had eggs."

"Where's the victim?" the first cop asked us, looking at the large puddle of blood.

I shrugged. "We don't know."

"He *left*?" the last cop to the scene asked, looking at the big bloodstain.

"Yeah," we said.

"Couldn't have gotten very far," the first guy said to the second pair of cops. "Which way did he go?" he asked Keith and me. We pointed, but something told me they wouldn't find the guy.

"You take it," he said to the team of cops who arrived after he did. "I'll stay with the kids and get what I can from them." He turned to his partner. "Call the mobile crime unit. Get them out here, okay?" he barked.

His partner nodded and headed back to the car. He talked into to the radio on his shoulder as he walked. "We need a mobile crime unit at the corner of . . ." was all I heard before the officer in front of me started asking questions.

"Who got hit?" he asked. He took out a small pad and held his pen in place for my answer.

I couldn't help him much. "I don't know."

"Male? Female?"

"Male."

"Description?" he asked.

I thought about it. "I don't know. Kind of tall. He looked pretty thin, but he must be built," I said.

"What makes you say that?" the officer asked, looking me deeply in the eyes.

"I could feel he was strong when he pushed me away from the car."

"So, he pushed you out of the way and took the hit himself?" the officer asked.

"Yeah." I realized just then that he could have taken those few valuable seconds to run away and save himself, but he hadn't. Instead, he'd used those precious moments to save me and get *me* out of the way.

The fact that he'd done that made me loyal to him, and for some reason, I didn't think I should tell the policeman about the day before or the flash drive.

"Anything else you want to add?" he asked.

"Yeah," Keith said. "Yesterday . . ." He started to blurt everything out. I couldn't let that happen.

"Yeah," I said, looking at Keith. "We were just saying that yesterday, I didn't have any breakfast, so I wouldn't have barfed like this. I'm so embarrassed," I said, looking at Keith and hoping he got the hint to shut up.

The policeman laughed. "Don't worry about it, kid. You were in a trauma and you were scared. It happens to the best of us."

He was a nice guy, and I felt a little bad for lying to him, but something just told me not to say anything about the flash drive. "Thanks," I said.

"Do either of you remember anything about the car?" he asked us.

Keith looked at me before answering this time. It was okay that he answered this question, so I nodded very faintly.

"It was black," Keith said.

The officer looked at me to see if I agreed. "Yes, it was black."

"Big? Small? SUV?"

"It wasn't an SUV," Keith said. "It was medium. Plain black. No markings."

"Markings?" I asked my friend.

"Yeah. You know, anything to tell it from other cars," Keith said. He smiled and turned to the officer. "I watch a lot of *CSI* and *Law & Order*."

The officer smiled and nodded. "Good. Now, anything else you can tell me?" he asked us. "Number of passengers? Did you see the driver?"

Keith shook his head. "No. The windows

were tinted. Really dark. You couldn't see the people inside."

"Hm," the police officer said as he wrote that down. "I'd say that was a noticeable marking."

"You would?" Keith asked with excitement.

He nodded. "I'll need your names and addresses, please." He lifted his pen to write. "And if neither one of you was hurt, you don't have to go to the hospital or come down to the precinct with us," he added.

He took our info and looked up. "Your bus is here, boys," he said as he snapped his pad closed. He reached into a pocket and took out two business cards. "Call me if you think of anything else," he said as he handed us the cards.

"Will do, sir," Keith said as he grabbed his backpack.

For the second day in a row, it hurt to pick up my backpack.

I was hoping this wasn't a trend. I didn't know if my body could handle it.

CHAPTER
7

"That was weird, wasn't it?" Keith said. He was looking out the window at the police cars with their lights flashing. People were starting to crowd around. I noticed they were all stepping around the big pool of blood. I also noticed that the officers were not happy to have them trampling all over their crime scene.

"Weird?" I said. "*That's* the word you use for what just happened? 'Weird'?"

"Well it *was* weird," he said.

I stared at him. "Let me get this straight," I said in disbelief. "I lost my breakfast, and you just thought it was 'weird'?"

Keith nodded.

I couldn't believe it. "Seeing your school librarian at a grocery store? That's weird. Watching a two-hour show about sandwiches across America? And liking it? That's weird. Catching the principal picking his nose? That's weird."

"Mr. Newman picks his nose a lot," he said. "It's not that weird."

"All right. So forget the nose-picking-principal example," I agreed. "But the *other* things are 'weird,' right?"

"Right."

"And you think 'almost getting hit by a speeding car' fits in with those other things?" I asked. "In my opinion, that's *past* weird. That's . . . well, that's . . ." I couldn't think of a word that was bigger than "scary." Much bigger.

"Barfy?" Keith offered.

"Yeah," I said. "Scary enough to make ya puke."

Keith nodded. "I wonder if the guy got away safely."

I shrugged. "I don't know." Then I thought about things for a minute. "Do you think he's a good guy or a bad guy?" I asked. I was referring to the guy in the shiny shoes, but figured Keith knew that.

"I don't know. What do you think?" he asked me.

"No clue," I said.

School went okay. Nothing really happened until seventh period.

I was at my locker, getting my jacket and stuff so I wouldn't have to go all the way back there at the end of the day.

It saved me a lot of time when I just wanted to get out of school after a long day.

Anyhow, that's when John Larson came up to me.

"Here you go, man," he said. He shoved the flash drive into my hand and turned to leave.

"Did you find out what was on it?" I asked his back.

He turned around again and looked really nervous. "Um, no, man. Couldn't figure it out. I have *no* idea at *all* what is on that drive." He looked really tense. Like when your mother asks where you're going and you tell her you're going to the library to study.

Everyone knows you're not going to the library to study. How many people actually go to the library to study? Maybe I should rephrase that. How many people with C-minus *averages* go to the library to study? I'll even answer that for you. Including me? None.

Of course I was off to the arcade or going out for pizza. But I never had to hear anything about "wasting my money" or "ruining my appetite" when I said I was going to the library. In fact, my mom always got all mushy and smiley when

I told her I was going to the library. So since it made her so happy, I told her that a lot.

Someone who went to the library as often as I did should at *least* have a solid C. Or even a C plus! But my mother's never figured that out.

But just because *she* couldn't read that face, it didn't mean *I* didn't know the wearer of that look was lying through his teeth and feeling guilty about it.

"Come on, John. You can tell me. What's on it?" I pleaded.

"You don't know," he said firmly. "And it's best that it stays that way," he added quietly.

The way he said it made me very nervous. My mind was racing now. What could it be?

I looked at John, but he just shook his head and said, "You don't want to know, man."

Then he walked away.

That left me all worried and wondering. I don't think I heard one word said in eighth period. I was too busy trying to figure out what could be on that flash drive.

I kept checking my pocket to make sure it was still there. I'd put it in the pocket without the hole so I wouldn't lose it. But now that I knew it was *really* important—or dangerous—I was scared I'd lose it.

I kept picturing "shiny-shoes guy" dripping blood and hopping away. I heard his last words to me: *Keep that drive safe.* I pictured my leg all crushed and twisted. Bending in places that shouldn't bend.

I couldn't help but think that I was next. The guys in the medium-size black car with the tinted windows were going to get *me* next.

They really wanted whatever was on that flash drive. And shiny-shoes guy really didn't want them to have it.

So why did he choose me of all people to protect this thing?

Probably because they would have killed him for it if they'd found it on him.

I patted my jacket again, feeling the flash drive. And wouldn't you know it? I now had the thing!

This wasn't good. Not good at all.

I'm not a wimp or anything, but I really wasn't too happy to be walking around with something that caused people who had it to get their bones crushed.

The eighth-period bell rang just as I was trying to imagine what it felt like to get hit by a speeding car. It probably didn't feel so hot.

CHAPTER
8

When the bell rang, school was finally over. I thought it would never end.

I needed to talk with Keith. The flash drive had stuff on it that I probably shouldn't know about. I wasn't happy walking around school with it.

I got on the bus and waited for Keith to show.

When I saw his big, round face and his glasses poke into the doorway of the bus, I was more at ease. My backup had arrived.

Too bad Chad Lavario got on the bus right before him.

"Nice Band-Aid," Chad said with a loud laugh. He was pointing to my forehead so everyone would know what he was talking about.

Thanks, *Chad*, for pointing it out.

"You should see the giant *zit* under it!" Keith said, trying to explain my Band-Aid.

And thank you, Keith, for the extra help.

Keith was smiling at me as he sat in our assigned seat. "Hey," he said.

"Hey," I said back. Still a little ticked off.

He put his backpack on the floor by our feet. "You're not looking so good," he said.

I would have come back with a "gee thanks" or something, but I wasn't in the mood to joke around.

"You wouldn't look too good either if you'd talked with John," I said quietly. I didn't want anyone else to hear us talking. No use getting anyone else in danger. It seemed to me that the less people who knew about the flash drive, the better.

"What did he say?" Keith asked.

I shook my head. "It's not good."

"Did he find out what's on it?" he asked.

I looked Keith in the eye. "Well, that's the thing. I think he *does* know what's on it. But he wouldn't tell me."

"Why not?"

"He said I don't want to know."

Keith made a face. "Eww. That doesn't sound good."

"Yeah. I know."

"What else did he say?"

I lowered my voice. "He said that it's best if I didn't know what was on it."

Keith's face lit up. "You mean so when they torture you, you can't give them any answers?" He looked so excited.

"How can you be excited about my getting tortured?" I was getting angry. "You know, I wouldn't be excited if it were *you* getting tortured."

Keith looked upset. "Sorry. It was just that I felt like we were in the movies for a second there."

"Yeah, well, like I keep telling you . . . it's all fake in the movies. This is real, Keith! It'll be my *real* blood spurting out. My *real* bones getting crushed. My *real* head being smashed."

Just then the bus swerved to the right and I found myself squooshed up against Keith. "Sorry, dude," I said, trying to push myself away from him. I was so close, I could see the pores on his face. I didn't want anyone to think I was, you know, going in for a kiss or anything, so I looked around.

Everyone else was having the same problem.

Mrs. Sewers was driving like a maniac. It was very unlike her. You know, with her whole perfect safety record and all.

Just then, Mrs. Sewers made a sound that didn't sound human.

The entire bus went quiet.

She was a gruff old lady . . . but up until one second ago, I'd always thought she was at least, you know, human.

"Are you okay, Mrs. Sewers?" I called to her.

"Some idiot is trying to run me off the road."

I looked out the bus windows. So did Keith. We looked out all around the bus. Left. Right. Front and back. All around us were black sedans.

I heard Keith mutter, "Oh, my God."

I felt inside my pocket. The flash drive was still there.

"What's on that thing?" he asked me.

"I don't know," I said.

"What is *on* that thing?" he repeated louder. He reached up and grabbed my coat with both hands. He started shaking me.

"Hey," I said, trying to make him snap out of it before he broke my neck. He was frantic. "Hey!" I said louder.

When he still kept shaking me, I screamed, "HEY!"

He stopped right away and said, "I'm so sorry, Al. It was like I was in a trance or something."

I pushed his hands off of me. "Get a grip, dude!" I yelled at him.

"Whatever it is, it must be important," he said. His eyes looked wild. Like he was a trapped lion.

"Yeah," I agreed.

The bus sped up and was veering left and right. Mrs. Sewers was all over the road.

"Hang on, kids," she said really loud. It sounded like she was using a bullhorn, but she wasn't. It was her own natural voice. "It looks like we've picked up a few more idiots. I'm trying my best to get away from these clowns."

Clowns? She thought these guys in the black sedans were clowns?

I had news for her. They weren't clowns. They weren't the *least* bit funny! They were serious. Very serious. And dangerous.

"We're in deep doo-doo, aren't we?" Keith asked.

"Yeah, I think we are," I said. I felt like I was going to be sick.

The bus swerved to the left, and Tamika Greenberg fell out of her seat right into the aisle.

Mrs. Sewers saw her in that long mirror above the windshield. Normally, Mrs. Sewers would have gotten all bent out of shape over that. But she was too busy trying to keep the bus on the road.

"Try to stay in your seats, kids. Are you okay, Tamika?" she asked.

"Yes, Mrs. Sewers," Tamika said. "Glad I didn't wear a skirt today," she added.

Some people laughed, but to be honest, most of us were too scared to laugh at a joke. It just wasn't the time for fooling around. We were speeding down the road, weaving in and out of traffic in a big yellow school bus.

I mean, Mrs. Sewers may have a great safety record, but Mario Andretti, she's not!

"What's up with these fools?" Mrs. Sewers said out loud.

She was starting to slow down, which was a very bad idea.

"Keep going, Mrs. Sewers," I said loudly. I was trying to think of a good place to hide the flash drive. Just in case the men in the black cars overtook the bus.

It was a good possibility. It was four against one. Four easy-to-maneuver cars against one big, clunky old school bus.

I thought about slipping the flash drive to Tamika Greenberg, but I didn't want to put her—or anyone—in danger.

Take my word . . . it was scary being in danger.

CHAPTER

9

I tried to think what Vin Diesel would do if he were me.

Besides being shocked that he had *hair*, I think his first move would be to smash out the bus windows with his bare fists.

Okay. That one wasn't going to happen.

Then, he'd jump out of the racing bus, landing on a motorcycle.

I looked around. Not a motorcycle in sight, thank God. Not that I would've tried doing a trick like that. Knowing me, I'd be speaking soprano until I was *sixty* if I jumped out of a bus onto a motorcycle.

Okay. Then he'd hot-wire the motorcycle, of course. In less than thirty seconds. Sadly, I don't have hot-wiring ability. So that rules *that* out.

And then he'd take off in a cloud of gravel. I could probably manage that. But not too easily, without a motorcycle. Or *any* vehicle. Maybe I could just pick up some gravel in my bare hands and throw it.

So. I'm not Vin Diesel. I'm Alfonse Netti.

And at the moment, Alfonse Netti was hanging on to the back of the seat in front of him like a wuss. I also was trying to think of a place to hide the flash drive.

I finally thought of a place.

There was a small tear in the green vinyl of our seat. Sometimes I stuck my finger in there, just for fun.

Other times, I found tiny gum wrappers stuffed in there.

Today, there were wrappers.

So I pulled them out and tried to shove the drive in there.

It wouldn't go all the way in.

I shoved harder, but it wouldn't fit.

The bus was still swerving all over the road, and I ended up sliding out of my seat. In Tamika's and my defense . . . those suckers are slippery.

Keith pulled me back up into the seat.

Again I tried to shove the flash drive into the hole, but it wouldn't stay. I had to think of something else.

I thought and thought but couldn't come up with anything. I thought of Vin Diesel again and got depressed. I knew he was an actor and only did what the writers told him to do. I mean, the guy probably didn't even think of his moves himself. But I was nothing like Vin Diesel. Nothing!

I mean, I bet Vin Diesel never got scared (even

in a *real* crisis). And I bet Vin Diesel wasn't a big wimp. (No matter what the writers wrote for him to act out.) And I bet that Vin Diesel never got giant, Mount Fuji-size pimples. (*No* amount of makeup could cover this sucker up.) And if Vin Diesel *did* get pimples, I bet he didn't wear Band-Aids over them.

No. Vin Diesel wore his wounds—and his pimples—proudly. He didn't care what anyone thought. His eyeball could be hanging from a vein, and he wouldn't be ashamed. No. Not Vin Diesel.

If he saw (out of his good eye) that someone was looking at him funny, he'd get in their face and scream, "What are *you* looking at?"

I thought of my monster pimple and the Band-Aid I'd slapped on it this morning. I'd been trying to cover it—well, hide it, really—but I had an idea. A great idea! A Vin Diesel idea. A *better* than Vin Diesel idea, because Vin Diesel wouldn't wear a Band-Aid.

Oh, well. His loss.

I bravely ripped the Band-Aid off my forehead. DANG!!! That hurt. "Dang it!" I screamed.

I was holding the Band-Aid in my hand. It was dangling from my fingers.

"Gross, dude! What *are* you doing?" Keith said. He was staring at my forehead. "The bus is totally out of control and you're playing with your *pimple*?"

I looked around. Everyone was upset. And Mrs. Sewers was driving her heart out.

"I wish that girl would stop screaming," I said. "I can't think with that noise."

Keith laughed. He actually laughed. "That was you screaming, Al."

"No, it wasn't," I said, trying to look as tough as Vin Diesel.

I guess I didn't pull it off. "Sure was, dude! The only one screaming around here is you. You've been screaming like a girl for the last five minutes."

"I have?" I couldn't believe that.

"Yeah. But take my word: It was only about five minutes, but felt like two hours."

I blushed. "Sorry, man. I'm just thinking about the guys in the black cars. I've seen their work, and I'm a little nervous."

"Ya think?" Keith said with a grin.

He was looking at my pus-covered Band-Aid.

"Now's not the time to scale Mount Fuji," he said loudly.

Great. Now everyone would know we called my pimple Mount Fuji.

Again, I thought of Vin Diesel. I knew he most likely never got pimples. But if he *did*, I wondered if he'd name them. Most likely not.

I took my pus-filled Band-Aid and used it to tape the flash drive under the seat. That had been my great idea.

"There!" I said, pleased. Maybe I had a little Vin Diesel in me after all.

Of course, right after that, the flash drive fell down with a clink.

"It's too heavy for the Band-Aid," I said aloud.

I thought, *I should probably find another Band-Aid*.

I looked around.

CHAPTER
10

Harold Glick had Band-Aids all over his hands. He worked at the local deli and had a hard time trying to keep his fingers out of the slicer.

Last time I was in there, some guy was yelling at Harold, "I asked for a *HAM* sandwich, not a *HAND* sandwich!"

It was hard enough doing that kind of work. But dealing directly with the public? That could be brutal.

I mean, look at the abuse Harold Glick had to take.

I know if *I'd* just cut my hand for the millionth time and some obnoxious guy yelled at *me* like that, I'd be forced to jump over the counter to kick his sorry butt.

Yeah, right. I know. I should keep dreaming.

I looked at Harold and felt bad for what I had to do next. But . . . duty called.

The bus was still rocking and rolling. So I stumbled back four rows and faced Harold head-on.

"Sorry, dude," I said right before I ripped off one of his Band-Aids.

I hoped I'd picked a less important one. I wouldn't want Harold's finger falling off or anything.

"Ow!" Harold cried out. "What did you do *that* for?"

"Sorry, dude," I said again. "But it's an emergency."

Harold stared blankly at me. Good thing he was used to dealing with the public and was used to people saying and doing obnoxious things to him. Or I'd be in big trouble.

My mind wandered.

I pictured the results of ripping a Band-Aid off Vin Diesel. I probably wouldn't live to tell the tale. But . . . I was safe. Vin Diesel didn't wear Band-Aids. And Harold Glick was nothing like Vin Diesel. Well, except Harold will probably be as bald someday. But take my word, Harold won't look as cool as Vin Diesel. Trust me. I've seen Harold's father. The man's as bald as a cue ball. And it doesn't look cool on Mr. Glick like it does on Vin Diesel.

I was walking back to my assigned seat when the bus took a sharp turn to the right. I almost fell on Leslie Mortina. That wouldn't have been a bad thing. She's the hottest girl in school. And not just based on *my* list. I think she was at the top of the list for *every* guy at school.

As pleasant as falling on Leslie Mortina would be, I had urgent business to get to. I didn't have time to fall on a gorgeous blonde. After all, the bloody Band-Aid I took from Harold Glick wasn't going to stick the flash drive to the bottom of my assigned seat by itself. Which was too bad. Because that was the closest I'd ever gotten to Leslie Mortina.

But now I had an excuse to talk to her. Cool!

"You okay?" I asked Leslie.

"Yeah," she said, looking grossed out. She was gazing at Harold's bloody Band-Aid in my hand.

Like I always say, there's nothing like making a good first impression.

"It's for a good cause," I said, waving the Band-Aid toward my seat.

She rolled her eyes and sat back in her own assigned seat. I was dismissed.

That hurt. Deep. I'd just been snubbed by Leslie Mortina.

It was the first time. But with any luck, it wouldn't be the last time. God, she smelled good. And that hair? Gorgeous.

I finished taping the flash drive under my seat. Now that that was done and the drive was safely hidden, I stumbled up to Mrs. Sewers.

"How's it going up here, Mrs. Sewers?"

She was still driving like a lunatic, and sweat was beading all over her old, wrinkly face. Her small, beady eyes flashed in my direction.

"Stay behind the yellow line, Mr. Netti," she barked.

Ever since the first day I had the lady as my bus driver, we had been on a formal basis. She never called me Alfonse or Al. It was always "Mr. Netti."

"You're doing a great job staying away from those guys," I said. I was trying to be nice to her. I thought it was the smart thing to do. Because when she found out the guys in the four black cars were after *me*, I figured she'd go ballistic. That, plus she'd hate me forever.

You don't want your bus driver to hate you forever. You'd end up assigned to sit next to the weird guy with the bad gas problem.

"I wish I knew what they wanted," she said. I thought I heard her growl. That was scary.

"Beats me," I said innocently. I think I said it too innocently, because her beady little eyes were boring right into me. They were like two laser pens, burning holes in me.

"Well, I'm sorry, kids, but I'm not stopping this bus. And no one's getting *off* the bus either. Not until I lose those goons," she said loudly. "And *get behind the yellow line*, Mr. Netti," she roared. "Better yet . . . *all of you get your butts in your assigned seats!*"

She was screaming. Out of control. But I understood. She was tense. The bus was really cooking now. This was the fastest I'd ever seen a bus go. A school bus, that is. I saw that movie *Speed* with Sandra Bullock. You know the one. With the bus that had to keep going over fifty miles per hour or it would blow up? So I knew regular buses could go kind of fast. But a school bus? I had no idea these big, yellow babies could cook like this.

Mrs. Sewers had steered the bus onto the highway, and we were cruisin'!

It was like NASCAR. Only with a big, old bus. And Mrs. Sewers at the wheel. Like I said, she wasn't Mario Andretti, but she was close.

Mrs. Sewers was holding her own. There she was, clutching that big, round steering wheel like there was no tomorrow.

I was thinking, if the guys in the four sedans got her to stop the bus, for me there might not *be* a tomorrow.

With that thought in mind, I said, "Keep going, Mrs. Sewers."

"Sit *down!*" she yelled back.

Just then we hit a tight curve.

CHAPTER

11

I could tell Mrs. Sewers was doing her best to keep the bus on the road. But that curve was too sharp.

I never thought this could happen on a bus, but we were taking the curve on two wheels. If we weren't getting chased by people looking to kill me, I would have thought that was really cool.

Mrs. Sewers screamed, *"Get in your assigned seats, people. And prepare for the worst!"*

The bus was screeching out of control. We were sliding sideways.

She was trying really hard to make the curve, but the bus was out of control.

"It was nice knowin' ya," Keith said to me.

He looked scared out of his wits.

So, he wasn't the big tough guy he thought he was. Was he?! And maybe now he'd realize that I'd handled things pretty well so far.

It was different when your own butt was on the line, *wasn't* it?

"Don't worry, Keith," I said back. "Everything will be fine."

Just then the bus lurched out of control and started sliding toward a group of trees.

"Or not," I said. I tried not to shrug but couldn't help myself.

"Hang on, kids. We're gonna crash!" Mrs. Sewers yelled.

I was afraid the tree branches would break through the windows. But I'd wasted my time

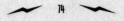

worrying about that. I should have been worrying about what really happened.

The bus tipped over and ended up sliding, sideways, into the bank of trees.

I should probably mention that I was lying on top of Keith, and someone was on top of me, but I couldn't tell who. They were covering my face.

My first thought was that I'd hoped it wasn't anyone's butt.

I must have been in shock because I was just lying there, dazed and confused. But then all heck broke lose. Kids were screaming and crying. And I found out it was Michael Supovich on top of me. He was smothering me with his chest and when I turned my head to breathe, I got a noseful of armpit. Hairy armpit. Smelly, hairy armpit. Ugh.

I shoved him off of me. "Ever heard of the word 'deodorant'?" I said as I pushed.

"What?" Larry Greer asked. He was above me too.

Well, actually, he was on top of Michael Supovich, who was on top of me. And we *all* were on top of Keith.

"Whoa, buddy," I said to Keith. "You okay?"

"I guess," he said. "It really hurts."

"Not too much fun, huh," I said, remembering the way he'd laughed at me after I got run over by Mr. Shiny-shoes.

That reminded me. I twisted around and looked under the seat for the flash drive. Yup, it was still there. The Band-Aid idea had worked.

"Everyone go out through the rear exit," Mrs. Sewers was shouting.

The bus was on its side, so we couldn't get out through the door. And we'd have to jump up to get through the windows. Plus, not many people could fit through those windows anyhow.

"Exit through the rear of the bus, people," Mrs. Sewers yelled. "If anyone is badly hurt, please shout out now."

There was lots of moaning and groaning, but no shouting. That was good.

"What if they're out cold?" someone called. "They can't shout out."

Everyone gasped, and the bus got quiet.

"Is someone unconscious?" Mrs. Sewers asked.

When no one answered, she said, "Look around, people, and see if anyone is knocked out."

Still no response.

"Answer me!" she yelled. Mrs. Sewers was losing it. I could relate. This was a nightmare. And I didn't even have a perfect safety record.

All the kids murmured that they were okay.

"All right, then, let's get off this bus," she ordered.

I thought of the flash drive safely Band-Aided to the bottom of my assigned seat.

"What will happen to the bus, Mrs. Sewers?" I asked.

"It'll be in the shop," she said. "For a long, long time," she added sadly. She looked around. "It might even be junked. It's an old bus, and there's a lot of damage."

I had to get that flash drive. If they ditched the bus, the drive would be trashed too.

I started fighting the flow to get back to my seat.

"Where are you going, Mr. Netti?" Mrs. Sewers demanded.

"I forgot something important," I said, still fighting my way through the crowd.

"This bus could blow," she said simply. "Nothing is that important."

Everyone was freaking out and started pushing and shoving to get to the back of the bus.

"Move it, moron," someone said.

Many people were heard saying, "Quit pushing."

"How are you doing with that door?" she

asked out loud. I guess whoever was back there had to open it first.

"It's stuck, but we're working on it," some girl said.

Then some guy said, "Um, Mrs. Sewers? There's a bunch of guys in suits all hanging around by the back of the bus. They don't look too friendly. And they don't look like they're Good Samaritans."

I felt like saying, "No! Don't open the door. They're bad. *Very* bad. They're bad Samaritans. And they're here to kill me." But I didn't say anything.

I really needed to get that flash drive. But I was also worried to have it on my body when I got off the bus.

"Um, Mrs. Sewers? We need to talk," I said.

"Not now, Mr. Netti. I'm a little bit busy at the moment," she responded.

"No, now's the right time. We need to talk."

CHAPTER
12

So. All of this was over that flash drive?" she asked. She looked around at the sideways bus and the panicked kids.

"Yes," I answered.

She looked closely at me. "What's on it?"

"I don't know."

"Where's the flash drive now?"

I pointed to my assigned seat. "I stuck it under my seat with Band-Aids."

She looked at my forehead. "That explains a lot."

What? Now she was a comedian? I almost told her not to quit her day job, but didn't think she'd laugh. Because of me she might get *fired* from her day job. So I thought I'd keep my cracks to myself.

"Okay, let's get it," she said to me. "Look out. Coming through," she said to everyone else.

We climbed around the seats until we got to my assigned seat.

"I see it," she said. "That silver thing, right?"

Was there something else taped under my seat with Band-Aids? I doubted it. "Yeah," I said. "That's it."

She ripped it off the bottom of the seat and handed it to me.

I pulled my hands back and didn't touch it. "I don't know if I should take it out there, Mrs. Sewers. They know what I look like."

Mrs. Sewers looked at me with those tiny, beady, laser-beam eyes. She could be scary sometimes. But, at the moment, the guys in the suits were scarier.

She kept her beady eyes trained on me as she pulled out her blouse. For a second there, I thought she was going to flash me. *That* would be scarier than the men in the suits!

She stuck the flash drive down the front of her blouse.

Oh God, no!

She wedged it right in there. Between her . . . well . . . you know.

"What are *you* looking at?" she barked.

I really didn't need people thinking I was staring at Mrs. Sewers's chest. "Nothing," I said, looking away.

I wondered if the flash drive would stay there. You know. In place. I also wondered if the men in suits would search everyone until they found what they were looking for.

"They wouldn't dare look there," Mrs. Sewers said.

Wow, it was as if she could read my mind.

While I was getting *way* too grossed out, someone got the back door open. The kids were piling out of the bus like rats jumping off a sinking ship.

The minute my face cleared the back exit, the men in suits came rushing up to the bus. They were like swarming locusts. And I was the target.

"Play dead," Keith yelled.

"*What?*" I said.

"Play dead, Al. They'll leave you alone. They can't kill a dead guy."

I shook my head. That's the best he could come up with? If death weren't pending, I would have jumped down from the bus and slapped him up the side of his head. I think that was—by *far*—the stupidest thing he'd ever said.

The guys were about to grab me when the sounds of sirens filled the air. Police, firemen, rescue workers, EMTs, you *name* it. They were there.

Next thing I heard was a *phft, phft, phft, phft, phft, phft* sound. The sun was blocked for a few seconds and it got really windy out all of a sudden.

I looked up, and there, hanging in the sky, was the coolest helicopter I'd ever seen. It was just sitting there. Hovering. Hanging above the bus like it was tied to a string. Like it was parked. In midair.

"Cool," Harold Glick said. His Band-Aid-covered hand was shielding his eyes from the sun's glare.

"Wow," Leslie Mortina gushed.

"Yeah, wow," Tamika Greenberg said. "This is *so* cool."

The guys in suits ran back to their cars with their heads down low. As they drove off I noticed their cars didn't have license plates. Yeah, I *guess* they were unmarked cars.

The police didn't seem to notice because they were too busy worrying about the kids.

"Clear a space for the bird," a man on the helicopter's PA system called down to us.

Everyone started screaming and running around. It was like they were lunatics. Or possessed or something.

This group was definitely not good under pressure.

I don't know what made me do it, but I went over to Mrs. Sewers and said, "Please go stand over there in the woods." I pointed to the place I wanted her to go.

She looked at me. Hard.

"Why?" she asked.

"Helicopters need lots of space to land," I answered. "Because of the blades."

I could tell she was thinking about whether she should go or not.

"I know that from playing video games," I added.

A moment later, she nodded. Then she walked to the place I'd pointed to.

After that, I ran around from person to person telling them to go stand by Mrs. Sewers. Keith, too.

Once I herded everybody out of the way, the guy on the helicopter PA system spoke again. "Thanks, Al," he said.

The guy knew my name? How weird was that!

The helicopter started inching down and then landed.

CHAPTER
13

The blades slowed down as the engine was turned off. And we all watched as a door opened up.

Out came one shiny, black shoe. Followed by a crutch and a big white cast.

"Shiny-shoe man" slipped out of the helicopter. Then he hopped over to me and smiled. "Everyone here safe?" he asked.

"Yes," I said. I didn't know what else to say. I was surprised to see this guy again. It seemed like he was always there. No matter where or when.

I wondered how he knew where I was all the time. "How do you always find me?" I asked.

He laughed and shrugged. "The first time was a mistake. I had no idea who you were. You were just a body in the way."

I thought of how he had plowed into me that morning. "Gee, thanks."

He laughed again. "But then I needed to slip the drive somewhere. And you seemed as though you could handle it."

"I did?" That made me feel a little better.

He nodded. "Yes. And I was right," he said.

"How do you know my name?" I asked him.

"You were heading for school that morning. I just checked the bus records. It was easy," he said.

That made sense.

"And it was easy to find you the next day.

Same time, same place," he said with a smile.

I guess it *was* pretty easy to figure out who I was and how to find me, now that he'd said that.

"The next day, at your bus stop, I was very impressed with how you handled everything."

Everything? "You mean almost getting run down by a car?"

"Yes," he said, with a firm nod, as if that were a common thing to happen. "You were calm, cool, and collected. Very impressive, Al."

I smiled. "Thanks," I said, feeling proud.

He smiled back and nodded.

"So how did you find me today?" I asked.

He laughed. "Oh. That was easy. This chase was all over the police scanners. I figured . . . it had to be you. And them," he said. He pointed behind me with his chin.

I looked over my shoulder. The cops were bringing the guys in suits back to be identified by the shiny-shoes guy.

"Are these the guys, Agent?" the officer asked the man.

Agent? The man in the cast looked over the men in the suits. Totally unafraid. "Where's the fat, bald guy?" he asked the criminals.

"He's not here," one of them said. I could tell he was tough. A real wise guy, too.

"I see that. Where is he?!" the agent demanded.

No one spoke.

"I *said*"—he raised his voice—"where *is* he?"

"He's dead. You shot him in the alley," one criminal said with anger. He looked like the youngest of the bunch. And I could tell he wasn't the smartest.

He was rewarded with two elbows in his ribs and dirty looks from all the other criminals. "Shut up," a few of them whispered.

"That's okay," the agent said to the young hood. "Thanks for the info. Again." Shiny-shoes—or should I say "shiny-*shoe*"—winked at him as if the young guy helped him out all the time.

"Hey, I've never ratted out anyone," the young guy said to his buddies.

"Yeah, it's our little secret," the agent said to him with a big wink.

The way the suit-men were looking at the young guy, I could tell the young guy wasn't going to be around long enough to prove that he was telling the truth. I kind of felt sorry for the young guy. Shiny-shoe man just fried his butt.

I guess what my mom says is true: You should pick your friends wisely. The young guy hadn't picked his friends wisely. He was hanging with a tough crowd. They weren't going to cut him *any* slack.

The police took the handcuffed men to their squad cars. They peeled out soon after. My guess was they were going to get locked up. For a long time.

"Now," the guy in the cast said to me, "about that flash drive."

"It's right here in the bus," I said.

The man hopped behind me.

"Oh, wait a minute," I said. "I forgot. I moved it." I know that sounded weird, but let's not forget: I'd taken it from a good, safe place and given it to my old, frightful bus driver so she could keep it between her . . . well . . . you know.

The man waited. He just looked at me, and I got a little nervous. After all, if the bad guys were afraid of him, I guessed I should be too. "It's in between my bus driver's . . . um . . ." I didn't know how to finish.

"Your bus driver's what?" he asked.

Again, I didn't know how to explain. So instead, I waved my hands in front of my chest.

Shiny-shoe guy laughed out loud.

I realized I must have looked like an idiot. "I had the drive safely tucked away under my seat.

I used Band-Aids," I informed him. "But then the guys in the black cars came, and I was afraid they'd find it."

"Good thinking," he said. "So you hid it again?"

"Yes," I said, nodding.

"In your bus driver's . . . ah . . . 'chest area.'"

I couldn't help myself. I smiled. "Yeah."

"Does she . . . *know?*" he asked slowly. He looked like he was afraid to hear my answer.

"Of course she knows!" I said.

He threw back his head and laughed. "Well . . . would you mind *getting* it for me?"

I pictured myself taking the flash drive from its hiding place. I shuddered with disgust.

Of course I had to walk over to Mrs. Sewers to get the drive.

The man in the cast was right behind me.

Everyone was watching what was going on. Which was horrible. Because everyone was watching as Mrs. Sewers spread open her blouse, reached in there, came out with the flash drive, and handed it to . . . me.

As if *that* wasn't bad enough. What was *really* gross was that it was warm!

Like a hot potato, I gave it to shiny-shoe man.

He nodded and thanked me. "Great hiding place," he said.

"Yeah. No one would want to look in there!"

"You did a great job, Al. Maybe when you're old enough to recruit, you'll keep us in mind. We'll be keeping our eye on you, son."

"We?" I asked, wondering who "we" was.

"The agency, Al. We'll be watching you," he said with a wink.

Just then, another black sedan sped onto the scene. A guy got out of the passenger side, whipped out a machine gun, and started shooting.

Bullets sprayed everywhere. But that was just to get everyone to lie down. His *target* was

the agent. And, sadly, he hit his target. But not before the agent once again shoved me clear of danger.

I watched with horror as the man who'd saved my life—twice—went down like a sack of potatoes. I heard him groan a couple of times with each hit, and then he toppled over. Dead.

In a state of panic—or delirium—I took it upon myself to finish the job this man had started. His hand was still clutching the flash drive. But I pried his fingers open and grabbed it.

Then I looked around and saw that the police were busy taking down the shooter. He was on his stomach, and his hands were cuffed behind his back. But his eyes were what I noticed the most. They were trained on me.

And he gave me a look that said, "You're next."

CHAPTER
14

I had to get out of there. Now.

This agent *died* for that flash drive. And he'd saved me—twice. I had no idea what was on the drive, but I felt as if I needed to keep it safe.

The place was now more chaotic than it was when the bus crashed or when the helicopter landed.

"Keith!" I screamed. "Keith, where are you?"

"I'm here, Al," Keith said from a distance.

"We need to get the heck out of here," I called to him.

"I'm with ya, dude," he called back. I saw him running over to me. He was hunched over and running in a zigzag.

"What are you *doing*?" I asked him when he was close enough to hear me talk without shouting.

"Avoiding any bullets. In case someone starts shooting again."

That was so stupid, I had half a mind to shoot him myself. "We need to get out of here," I said.

I grabbed his collar and pulled him into the woods.

We ran in the woods for what seemed like hours. I don't know how we did it, but we managed to get back to town.

"What are you going to do now?" Keith asked me.

"I need to see a man about a drive," I said.

Keith laughed and shook his head. "If you

had to go, you should have gone in the *woods*, Al."

I rolled my eyes. "Not a man about a horse, you idiot. A man about a drive. I'm talking about John. John Larson. I don't care if he doesn't *want* to tell me what's on this drive. He's *going* to."

I stopped at a phone booth. "Are you going to call him?" Keith asked.

"No, I'm looking up his address," I said as I flipped through the phone book pages.

There were two Larsons in town. Keith and I left the phone booth and headed to the address that I thought was John's.

I was right.

"Hey, Al. What are *you* doing here?" he said all friendly like.

"Look, John. I'm not playing with you. I need to know what's on that drive." Police and ambulance sirens were howling in the distance. Getting closer. *"Now!"* I roared.

John paled. "Okay, Al," he said as he walked

out of his house and closed his front door. He nodded at the door. "I don't want my mother to hear."

"Whatever," I said. "Just spit it out. I need to know."

John looked around nervously. "They're plans for every dam and waterway in the U.S."

I was expecting more. Or maybe something different. "So? What's so secretive about that?" I asked.

John looked around again. "There's also detailed info on the structural weak spots of each dam," he whispered.

I still didn't get it. "Your point?"

"A few well-placed plastique devices—"

"You mean *bombs*?" Keith interrupted.

"Yes," John said quietly. "A few well-placed bombs, and our entire country will be in chaos."

Keith and I stared at John. We just weren't seeing what he was seeing.

"You thought Katrina was bad?" John asked us. "That was a *natural* disaster. And just in one place. Now picture hundreds of incidents like that. Across the country. All at the same time." He looked at us.

"That would bring *total* chaos," I said, more to myself than anyone else.

"Plus, it will break our nation financially as well as physically," John added.

I took it all in. "So who wants it? Who are these guys in the black cars?" I asked.

"I don't know," John said. "But based on what's happened so far, you don't have to worry about finding them. They'll find you."

"Yeah," I said. "That's what I'm afraid of."

"Yeah," Keith said. "Me too."

"You've got to help us," I said to John.

He shook his head. "No offense, guys. But I want no part of this. You're on your own." He went back into his house, and I heard him lock his door with finality.

Keith and I looked at each other.

"What are we going to do now?" Keith asked.

I shrugged. "We don't have time to contact every dam and waterway," I said. "You know, during Katrina I kept hearing about this 'U.S. Army Corps of Engineers' over and over."

"Who are they?" Keith asked

I shrugged again. "I don't know. Let's go to the library and look it up."

When we got to the library, we passed the pay phone in the entryway.

"I'd better call my mom," I said. "Got a quarter?"

Keith gave me a quarter.

"Hey, Mom? I'm at the library. Look, don't hold dinner, okay? I'm working on a project and it'll be a while."

"What did she say?" Keith asked when I hung up the phone.

"She's all happy," I said with a grimace. "At least I'm not lying to her for once."

"You didn't tell her about the whole bus shoot-out thing," Keith said.

"I will. But not now. She'd make me come right home, and I don't have time for that."

"Good thinking," Keith said as we entered the main part of the library.

I sat at a computer and googled "U.S. Army Corps of Engineers."

"Hey look, Keith. There's an 800 number listed. Let's call them."

We went back out to the entryway and used the pay phone.

"Hello. Is this the U.S. Army Corps of Engineers?" I asked the lady who answered the phone.

"Yes, it is," she said curtly.

"Good. Look. We don't know *who*, but we know some guys are going to blow up all our waterways," I said.

The woman gasped. "That is *not* funny, young man! Do you know you can get *arrested* for pulling a prank like this?"

"It's not a prank, and I'm not *trying* to be funny," I said.

"Well, you're not funny. Do not call here again, young man, or I'll have the phone traced and will have you arrested. Do you understand?"

"But . . . ," I said.

"No buts about it!" she said. "In fact, I've already started a trace."

That scared me for some reason, and I slammed down the phone.

I explained to Keith what just happened.

"Now what?" he asked.

"I don't know. Let me think."

I thought for a few moments. "Follow me," I said.

We went back to the main part of the library.

"If there's an 800 number for the U.S. Army Corps of Engineers, there's probably an 800 number for the CIA," I said.

"Good thinking," Keith said, impressed.

Problem was, there was no 800 number for the CIA. But I did get a number.

"Come on," I said. "Let's go."

"What are you going to do?" Keith asked.

I smiled. "You'll see."

CHAPTER
15

You have a collect call from . . . what did you say your name was, son?" the operator asked.

"Al," I said proudly.

"You have a collect call from Al," the operator said to the woman who answered the CIA's phone.

"I'm sorry. We don't accept collect calls," the lady said before hanging up with a *click*.

"Sorry, Al," the operator said. "Can I try anyone else for you today?"

I was desperate. "Look. This is important. I need to get through to the CIA. Please try again. But this time, give them my whole name, okay?"

"Okay, Al," she said cheerfully. If she knew how much danger she was in, she'd knock that cheerful note right out of her voice. "What's your full name?"

"Alphonse Netti."

"Okay, Al. Let's try again," she said happily.

When the same CIA lady answered the phone again, the operator said, "You have a collect call from a Mr. Alphonse Netti."

I liked the way she added the "Mr." part so I sounded more important.

"I'm sorry. We don't accept collect calls," the CIA lady said before hanging up with a click. What was she? A parrot?

"I'm sorry, Al. What now?" the operator asked.

She was very nice and I didn't want to yell at her, but I *really* needed to get through to the CIA. "Look. I know it's asking a lot. But can you try again and let me talk?"

She chuckled. "Sure, why not."

I heard the phone ring again. When the CIA lady picked up, I jumped right in. "I'm the guy who's going to blow up the dams across the nation," I blurted out.

"Please hold," said the CIA lady.

Some old guy got on the phone. "You *bastards*! We know your plans and are looking for you!"

"Um, it's not them. I'm Al. Alphonse Netti, sir. And I'm calling from—"

The operator broke in. "He is trying to reach you collect. Do you accept the charges?" she asked.

"Yes, yes. Sure," the old guy said.

"Good luck, Al," the operator said.

"Thanks," I said to her. Then I told the old man what had happened at the bus-crash site.

"Did they get the drive?" he asked.

"No," I said. "I have it."

"Good job, Al," he said. "We've been following these guys for months. We got a tip from our agent in Belgium. A European cell of Aquaris is planning this attack. But we don't know much. The clues have come in bits and pieces. But Agent Mansfield got his hands on the drive while it was being passed from the snitch to the first cell."

"Is that the guy who got his leg smashed and was, um, shot?" I asked.

"Yes," the old man said.

"I *knew* he was a great guy. He saved my life. Twice," I said.

"Sounds like Mansfield," the old man said with a chuckle.

I was thinking that "Mansfield" just got killed. Why would the old man laugh about *anything* that had to do with him? But before I could think my thought through, the old man spoke again.

"Aquaris got wind that we got a hold of the

drive. They called in all their people to get it back. You kids are lucky you're still alive. These guys play hardball. So keep that drive safe. I've got agents heading your way now. So hang tight. Where are you?" he asked.

I looked at Keith. "I don't want to tell you in case your line is tapped. I'm in a safe place, and the drive is safe." I hung up.

"Where *is* the drive?" Keith asked.

I looked south. "In my briefs."

"That can be dangerous," Keith said, talking about the knife-like shape.

"Yeah. Tell me about it," I said, making a face.

Keith laughed.

"Look," I said. "There's nothing we can do right now. Let's go home, eat dinner, and I'll meet you at McDonald's in the morning. *Don't* go to the bus stop, Keith. Get it?"

"Yeah, I get it. We'll meet at Mickey D's," he said.

• • •

From McDonald's, Keith and I could see the parade of black, unmarked cars with tinted windows driving up and down the street. After the school bus came and went—without us on it—the black cars started to leave.

"Okay, Keith. It's safe to go now," I said.

"What? So now we have to *walk* to school?" he griped.

"Would you rather have waited at the bus stop and gotten your *knees* blown off?" I asked as we left McDonald's.

We only went about eight steps when I heard a screeching sound. I turned to see a black sedan coming out of a small alleyway. It was headed right for us.

"Dang," Keith said. "One of the terrorists must have stayed behind."

"Ya think?" I asked him as we ran for our lives.

We ducked down a side street and heard the car's tires screech as it turned to follow us.

"Where should we go?" Keith asked.

"I don't know. But we should stick together," I said.

"I was thinking maybe we should split up," Keith said.

I looked over at my best friend. "Thanks."

"Sorry," he said around huffs of air. "I'm just freaking out a little."

"Yeah," I said, running my butt off. "I am too."

I grabbed Keith's shirt and pulled him up another side alley. It brought us right near that deli where Harold Glick works.

"Let's hit Harold Glick's deli," I said to Keith. "There must be lots of people around buying morning coffee."

"Good idea," Keith said as we slipped inside the deli.

"Hi, Mr. Dowd. Harold left something for school here and needs it so he doesn't get in trouble at school," I said. Boy, I was really thinking on my feet now.

"Why didn't he come and get it himself?" Mr. Dowd asked.

"Because he's in the classroom now," I said, trying to think something up.

"And he couldn't leave to get it or the teacher would know he didn't *have* it," Keith finished for me.

I nodded and smiled at Keith. "That was good," I whispered.

Keith shrugged. "You started it. I just finished it," he said.

We made a pretty good team sometimes.

"Go ahead and get it, boys," Mr. Dowd called to us.

I ran over to the cold-cuts section. I figured that's where Harold would leave something. Then I got an idea. "Hey. Let's shove the drive into one of those," I said as I pointed to the huge lumps of meat.

Keith laughed. "Okay. So what do you think? Ham or roast beef?"

"No. Not good," I said. "They may cut down to it if it's a big seller."

I turned to Mr. Dowd. "What's the slowest-moving item in the cold-cuts section?" I called to him.

Mr. Dowd laughed. "That would be either the olive loaf, the liverwurst, or the Limburger cheese," he called back to us.

"Thanks," I said to Mr. Dowd. I turned to Keith. "The cheese stinks, the liver stuff is *totally* gross, so it looks like it's the olive loaf."

"Looks like green eyeballs, doesn't it?" Keith asked as we looked at the olive loaf.

I rolled my eyes before I plunged the drive into the meat.

"There. How's that?" I asked.

"It left a hole," Keith pointed out.

I took an olive from the other side of the loaf and smashed it over the hole. "How's *that*?"

"Perfect," Keith said with a smile.

We left the deli, but not before Keith bought

us some Ring Dings, some sour cream-and-onion potato chips, and some soda.

"Ah," I said, clicking my soda can against Keith's as if I were saying a toast with a wineglass. "The breakfast of champions."

I spoke a little bit too soon, because I hadn't noticed a black sedan pulling up behind us.

In a flash, some big guys pulled us into the car and took off with tires squealing.

I don't know about Keith, but they put a cloth over my head so I couldn't see where we were going. When we got wherever we were headed, they pulled me out roughly and pushed me into a building.

They kept shoving me down a hallway until they pulled me into a room and pushed me onto a chair. They tied me up and took the cloth off my head.

Keith was sitting right next to me. Tied up in the next chair.

"Where's the drive?" a man with a funny

accent asked me. I couldn't place his accent. He sounded like a cross between James Bond and Pepé Le Pew.

I said nothing.

He took a long knife from his belt and ran his fingers over the side of the sharp blade. I think he was trying to give us a hint. "You'll tell us, or you'll never leave," he said seriously.

I don't know if it was due to nerves or the guy's silly accent, but Keith started to giggle.

The man looked ticked. I had to say something. "If you kill us, you'll never find out where the drive is."

"Yeah," Keith said. "We're more valuable to you dead than alive!"

"Keith!" I screamed at him.

Then he realized his mistake. "I mean, we're more valuable to you alive than dead."

I looked at Keith. "Why don't you just sit there and not talk, okay?"

Keith winced. "I'm nervous. I mess up when I'm nervous."

"All the more reason for you to just sit there and shut up," I said.

Another bad guy came in the room. This guy must be important because all the other bad guys treated him with respect. "What's going on?" the head bad guy asked.

"Nothing," one of the peon bad guys answered.

"Find out anything?" the head bad guy asked.

"No. Just that *this* one"—he pointed at me—"is the brains of the duo."

That brought big laughs.

I was insulted.

"Hey, I may not be very smart, but at least *I* know where the drive is!"

If I could have slapped my hand over my mouth, I would have. But both were tied to the chair at the moment.

The head guy kicked my chair and knocked me over backward. There I was, with my feet up in the air, my back to the floor, and my heart in my mouth. My big, *stupid* mouth.

The guy put his foot on my throat. "How about telling me where the drive is?"

I didn't speak.

"Or, I can crush your windpipe and you can then *show* me where it is."

I felt the bottom of his shoe press down further on my neck.

"Okay. I'll tell you," I said.

The head terrorist laughed. "You're not as dumb as you look, kid." He reached down and lifted me off the floor. By my hair. Dang, that hurt. Then he plunked me and the chair on the floor with a crash.

It was a good thing the drive was no longer in my briefs. I'd be in major pain by now.

"Untie them," the head terrorist said.

They did. And then they shoved Keith and me in a car.

"Where?" he asked.

"Go to town," I said. I was watching where we were driving. I wanted to tell the police their hideout.

As we drove, the men were talking in some strange language. The head guy turned to us and spoke. Only, it wasn't in English.

"Sorry," Keith said. "We don't speak Belgian."

The head guy got angry. "There's no such language as 'Belgian.'" He looked like this was a lesson he was sick of teaching.

"Oh," Keith said with wonder. "So what language *do* you people speak?"

"Flemish," he said tightly. He muttered the word "idiot" under his breath, but Keith was too far away to hear it.

"Shouldn't people who speak Flemish come from, you know, Flem?" Keith asked.

Everyone turned to stare at Keith.

"You know. Like people from Spain speak

Spanish and people from England speak English?" Then Keith got a thought. "Or maybe your country should be called Flemland."

One of the peon terrorists turned to the head guy. "Please, boss," he asked. "Can I shoot him?"

"Not yet," the boss said to the peon. "Now where?" he said to me.

I hesitated. I didn't want Mr. Dowd to get hurt.

The head guy turned in his seat and slapped my face. Wow, that stung.

"I'm sorry," I said quickly. "I have a bad sense of direction. I'm trying to remember."

The head terrorist shook his head. "These kids are *complete* idiots."

Oh. *That* he had to say in English.

We got to the deli, and we all burst in on Mr. Dowd as he was preparing for the lunch crowd.

"Hi, Al," Mr. Dowd called as he saw me.

The head guy shoved me forward. "Hi, Mr. Dowd."

Mr. Dowd's face clouded over when he saw all the thugs pour in behind me. "Are you all together?" he asked.

I moved my eyes left to right, left to right. I hoped he realized I was signaling the word no.

"Yes," the head guy said as he shoved me farther into the deli.

"Let me get some menus for you," Mr. Dowd said with a big smile. He walked to the register and felt around under the counter. Then he laughed nervously. "Oh. I forgot. My wife moved them. They're over there now," he said as he pointed to the place the menus always were. But the bad guys wouldn't know that. I was hoping he'd pressed some kind of alert button under the register or something.

He walked to the doorway and got some menus from the basket hanging by the door. I noticed he'd rubbed his shoulder across the door, moving the OPEN sign to CLOSED. But no one else noticed. They were too busy looking at me.

"Where is it, kid?" the head guy hissed quietly.

"It's in with the cold cuts, but I didn't put it there. Someone else did. The kid who works here. His name is Harold Glick," I whispered back.

The head guy turned to Mr. Dowd. "Do you have a kid named Harold Glick working here?" he asked.

"Yes, but he's in school right now. He's our sandwich maker," Mr. Dowd said.

The head guy nodded. "We're going to have to see those meats."

"But . . . ," Mr. Dowd started to protest.

"No buts, bud. We can either slice the meats . . . or you."

As if on cue, the rest of the thugs whipped out their knives. The head guy pulled out his gun.

He pointed it at Mr. Dowd. "You," he said. "Get over there." He motioned with his gun to the other thugs.

Mr. Dowd walked over to the knife-bearing bunch.

"You," the head guy said to me. "Start cutting up the meat." He waved his gun at me to make sure I did what he asked.

"Sure thing," I said. I took out the ham. "Would you like it thicker, thinnish, or shaved?" I asked.

He shot off a round that whizzed by my ear. "Stop playing with me and wasting my time," he said.

"Okay, then. Thicker it is," I said.

I picked up a knife and started cutting. The head guy didn't like that I had a knife. I knew that because he shot it out of my hand.

My hand was bleeding and hurt like you wouldn't believe.

"Use the machine," the head guy said, pointing to the slicer machine. You know the one. The one that cut Harold's hands to shreds.

"I'm not very mechanical," I said to the head guy. I hoped he'd change his mind.

Another shot rang out, and my left ear started to burn.

Keith screamed. "Oh, my God, Al. I think he just shot your ear off!"

I reached up and touched my ear. Blood covered my hand.

Oh, this was not good. Not good at all.

I got dizzy and felt like I was going to throw up.

"I just nicked you," the head guy said. "If I'd wanted to shoot your ear off, I would have. Now . . . *get* mechanical."

I flipped on the slicer machine with my good hand. It powered up as the blade whirred into motion.

"Now start slicing big, thick slices." The head guy pointed to the cold-cuts case with his gun. "Start with the meat on the left and move to the right."

Thank God the olive loaf was on the right-hand side of the case.

"Okay. You're the boss," I said.

I cut big slices of three roast beefs, four hams, and started working on the Swiss cheese.

"Forget the Swiss cheese," the head guy said.

"Okay," I said, placing it aside. I guess he figured he could see the drive through one of the holes in the cheese.

I did two *baked* turkey breasts next. Then I was on the first *smoked* turkey breast when the police crashed through the door. All heck broke loose.

Guns were firing, knives were flashing, and fists were making contact with flesh.

Had I not been right there, it would have been cool. But my butt was on the line.

In the distance I heard Keith screaming and I ran to him. I grabbed his shirt and pulled him over to the soda case. "Hide with me behind here," I said.

Mr. Dowd crawled on his belly over to us. "You guys okay?" he asked.

"I've been better," I answered.

Ten minutes later the place was *swarming* with cops and the bad guys were lying in pools of blood.

"Get this kid to a hospital," I heard a cop say right before I passed out.

When I woke up, I was lying in a hospital room.

A pretty nurse was hovering over me.

"Did I die? Am I in heaven?" I asked.

Then a *really* ugly nurse walked over, pushed me to my side, and tried to stick a thermometer in my, um . . . "Or am I in hell?" I said.

I rolled back on my back and pushed the ugly nurse away. "No *way!*" I said to her.

"Can you do that later, Nurse Schlitz?" some guy asked Ugly Nurse.

"Or not at all?" I added

When Ugly Nurse left the room, I turned to thank the guy who'd sent her away.

"Thanks, dude. That could've gotten *nasty.*"

Then I recognized him—more from the big cast on his leg than from his face. His face was a lot paler and more drawn than I recalled. He was wearing an ugly hospital gown and dragging some sort of machine. He must have been a patient like me. "Hey. It's you. You're *alive!*"

"Yes." He laughed. "It's hard to get rid of me."

"You're like a cockroach," I said.

"Thanks a lot," Agent Mansfield said with a chuckle. His chuckle ended in a wheezing cough.

"I didn't mean to insult you," I said. "Cockroaches can survive *anything*," I informed him.

"Then . . . thanks a lot," he said with a smile.

"I'm glad you're alive. Those guys were terrorists," I said.

"Yes, I know."

"They were trying to blow up the nation's waterways," I said.

"Yes, I know."

"That would have *totally* destroyed America!" I said with emotion.

"Yes, I know. I'm surprised you found out. You're very resourceful, Al."

I smiled. "Thanks." I saluted him, but then my hand hurt.

"No. Thank *you*, Al. Like I said, you'll make good agent material some day. We'll keep our eye on you. Today, you saved this whole country."

It was my turn to say, "Yes, I know." I was a little embarrassed by his praise. I think I even blushed.

I wondered if Vin Diesel got embarrassed like this.

"So where's that drive?" Agent Mansfield asked. "Back between your bus driver's, ah . . . ?" He left his question unfinished, then cracked up and shook his head.

"Nah. After I thought you were dead, I put it in my, um . . . briefs," I explained.

"Ew, that could have hurt," Agent Mansfield said, feeling the pain.

"Don't worry. I took it out before it did any damage."

He laughed. "Glad to hear that. So where is it now?"

"Stuck in a giant olive loaf. Hiding behind an olive."

He laughed again, and his machines started beeping loudly.

The pretty nurse came in and checked up on him.

"You lost a lot of blood, sir. You need to stay calm."

"Hard to do when you're around," he said to her with a wink.

"I can get Nurse Schlitz, if you prefer," she said with a devilish smile.

"NO!" he and I shouted together.

ONE LAST THING . . .

Someone once said that every living person will get fifteen minutes of fame at some point in his or her lifetime.

Mine was more like twenty seconds.

But, hey. I got it, I took it, and I sure did enjoy it.

Yesterday, television stations across the nation were talking about how some unnamed kid had saved the country from a terrorist attack.

Because of my age, they didn't name names.

But I was okay with that, because I didn't want any other bad guys coming after me.

Then, somehow, today, it got leaked at my school that I was that kid.

Everyone paid attention to me today, even Leslie Mortina.

It was great.

All of a sudden, I was really popular.

But like I said . . . it only lasted about twenty seconds.

At lunchtime, when I hit the boys' room, all the urinals were taken. So I went to a stall.

I'm right in the middle of, you know, things, when out of nowhere, I hear a familiar voice.

"So, Al. How do you like being famous?"

I looked under the next stall.

All I could see was one shiny black shoe and the bottom of a crutch.

"Are you the one who spread the news around here that it was me?" I asked Agent Mansfield.

He laughed. "Yup, sure did. You did a great job, Al. I just thought you deserved a little credit."

"Well, thanks," I said.

"No problem," he replied.

I didn't know what to say next, so there was a long pause.

"So how'd you and Keith like the new Vin Diesel movie last night?" he asked me.

Dang. They really *were* watching me.

TAKE A SNEEK PEEK AT AL AND KEITH'S NEXT ADVENTURE:
KILLER LUNCH LADY

"Look at her," Mike said softly.

He was still watching the lunch lady, Mrs. Holt.

She was waving that little metal box all around. She looked like a scarecrow waving in the wind. Or a hectic businesswoman trying to hail a cab.

It would have looked funny if it weren't so . . . bizarre.

"What *is* she doing?" Keith asked me.

I looked at my best friend. Why does he always think *I* know everything?

"I don't know, Keith. Do I *look* like her mother?" I asked him.

He shrugged. "I don't know. I've never seen her mother."

Roshni laughed. "If Al looks like Mrs. Holt's mother, then she's one butt-ugly woman."

"Can we *focus*, people?" Mike cried out. "There's something really wrong with this picture. Don't you think?"

Mrs. Holt was now running around. She looked like a chicken with her head cut off. Not that I'd ever *seen* a chicken with its head cut off. But I'd imagine it would be pretty funny.

She was sticking that metal box at each lunch table. Then she was looking at each kid. Hard. Like she was wondering if they were up to something.

"What *is* she doing?" I asked aloud.

I didn't expect an answer.

We watched as she quickly moved from table to table. She was trying to get whatever she was doing done by the time the Chris Vale chaos ended.

It *was* ending. So she was being more subtle

about it. But she was still doing it. Whatever "it" was.

"Maybe she's a spy," Keith said.

I rolled my eyes. "And what's she trying to do? See how many kids get sick from her cooking?"

"Can a metal box do that?" Mike asked.

"Maybe it's a vomit meter," Keith said.

"Do they *have* a vomit meter?" Mike asked Keith. "I don't think they have vomit meters."

As stupid as it came off, Keith was sticking with his whole "vomit meter" idea. "It's probably a high-*tech* vomit meter."

"Oh, yeah. That explains *everything*," I said. I couldn't stop my eyes from rolling.

I really liked my friends, but sometimes they were real morons.

"Well, what do *you* think she's doing?" Keith asked me.

"I don't know, for sure. But I think it's safe to say she's *not* metering vomit," I said.

Just then, Mrs. Holt passed her box thingie in front of Melissa Evans.

A little red light on the box started flashing like crazy.

THE HARDY BOYS

BOYS

UNDERCOVER BROTHERS™

They've got motorcycles,
their cases are ripped from the headlines,
and they work for ATAC:
American Teens Against Crime.

CRIMINALS, BEWARE:
THE HARDY BOYS ARE
ON YOUR TRAIL!

Frank and Joe are telling all-new stories of crime,

danger, death-defying stunts, mystery, and teamwork.

Ready? Set? Fire it up!

HAVE YOU FOUND ALL THE

SPYGEAR™

BOOKS?

BOOK 1:
The Secret of Stoneship Woods

BOOK 2:
The Massively Multiplayer Mystery

BOOK 3:
The Quantum Quandary

BOOK 4:
The Doomsday Dust

BOOK 5:
The Shrieking Shadow

BOOK 6:
The Omega Operative